Little Bits

A Collection of Short Stories

SARAH MAURY SWAN

Table of Contents

Preamble

Sometimes, writers temporarily run out of plotline for whatever book they're currently working on. Some of them take a break from writing and bake a cake or take a trip or anything other than the story.

My trick is to tickle my brain cells by answering "prompts." For instance, the owner of Next Chapter Books and Art, our wonderful local "indie" bookstore, sends out requests for each issue of *Next Chapter Literary Magazine*. I'm pleased to say I have published a story in each issue and then have moved back to working on my books.

However, now that the stories have been published once, they shouldn't just languish in a file on my computer, never to be seen again.

"Ah ha!" thought I. "Why not put out a book of these stories?

After another serious edit, of course. There is always room for improvement.

The second collection of stories will be some that have never been published. After all, it isn't the stories' fault that editors haven't wanted to publish them. I think I'll do a collection of stories featuring animals next, but, of course, I'll have to get the "writer's" polish to make them dazzle the reader's eye.

But I'm not Sick!

Illustration by Brooklynn Moore

The inaugural magazine, *Quarantine*, was the perfect theme for a story about something that happened when I was six-years-old and had just been uprooted from California to the Washington, DC area. My brothers, Richard and Bill, were already in the area and in a local summer camp.

The plan had been that they would stay there until my maternal grandmother, sister, Anne, and I arrived from Los Angeles. Then the boys would come home from camp.

Unfortunately, shortly after we arrived, Anne was put into isolation at the DC's Children's Hospital with polio. Which meant I was stuck inside our rental house looking out the window onto the streets of old town Alexandria, Virginia.

I remember things about the house, like the footprint in the cement hearth in front of the living room fireplace that was purportedly George Washington's. Of course, you could probably point out his footprint just about anywhere you go in our country.

I also remember going into the kitchen one time and seeing a strange man taking something out of the refrigerator. Turns out there was a whole different family living there. I wonder if any of them contracted polio.

My sister spent at least a month in the hospital, but never suffered any after-affects from her disease.

~

Sally's fire-red hair sparkled in the warm sun shining through the front window of this strange new house. People walked by. Why couldn't she?

"Sally, darling," her grandmother called from the doorway, "Come here for a hug."

Sally shook her head and headed to the front door. She stretched her slim fingers toward the door knob and looked back at her grandmother.

Granny said, "I'm sorry baby girl, but we still can't go out.

Sally stamped her foot and plunked herself on the floor. "I won't leave this door until we go outside."

Granny sighed, "It may be a long wait, Love."

Sally lips trembled and a tear slid down her cheek. "Why? What did I do bad?" She tried to smile, but her lips firmly turned downward. "I'm sorry. I promise not to do it again."

Granny pulled her granddaughter up, hugging her close. "You didn't do anything bad. Your sister is very ill. And you may have the same disease." She muttered to herself, "Six-year-olds shouldn't have to be quarantined."

"What's a disease?"

"Something wrong in your body. Anne has polio."

Sally snuggled closer to Granny. "Well, why aren't Bill and Richard here?"

"They were supposed to come home this week. But now they have to wait until Anne gets better.

Sally stamped her foot and wailed. "I want to go back to California. It was nice there."

Granny chuckled. "Sorry, but your mommy got a job here." She bent down to kiss Sally's head.

Sally kicked Granny in the shin and jerked back from her. "I don't want you to kiss me!" She reached for the doorknob again, but Granny yanked Sally back and smacked her bottom.

"That hurt! No cookies for you, instead you will go to your room and think about what you've done.

"Cookies?" Sally's face brightened and she wiped away her tears. "What kind of cookies?" She headed toward the kitchen.

One side of Granny's mouth curved up, but still she frowned. "No siree, not now. To your room!"

Sally dragged her feet on every step up to her bedroom. *Not fair*, she thought, *Richard and Bill are having fun at camp and Anne's having fun in the hospital, but I'm not having any fun at all.* When she got to her room, she grabbed her Raggedy Ann doll and unbraided its hair. But before she could re-braid it her eyelids drooped and the next thing she knew her mother called from downstairs.

"Sally! Sally! I'm home."

Raggedy Ann dropped to the floor as Sally jumped to her feet and raced downstairs. "Mommy, please can't I go outside?"

Mommy stroked Sally's face. "Tomorrow, darling girl. Tomorrow afternoon when I come from the hospital with Anne."

"Anne's all better?"

"At least she's well enough to come home. Your brothers will be home tomorrow also."

Sally danced around her mother. "Outside! Outside!" She squinted her eyes and stuck out the tip of her tongue. "Let's see. First, I'll play hopscotch." She shook her head. "No, let's all go swimming!"

Hearts' Convergence

The second issue's theme was **Convergence** since our town, New Bern, NC, sits on the joining of the Neuse and Trent Rivers. So, I wrote a brief romantic story about a teen boy thinking of the girl he likes as he kayaks down the Neuse toward where the Trent converges with it. Since my three novels are for children, I was trying to keep my short stories in that age range.

~

Charlie frowned as his reflection faded from the water's surface. Black clouds rushed to hide the sun, and the wind rocked his kayak. He rested the paddle across the hull and stretched his six-feet-five-inch frame up from his seat, wondering if, at seventeen, he'd finally quit growing. He hoped not. *I'd be happy with two more inches. Makes a difference in basketball.*

The boat waddled from side to side and pushed forward without his help. *What happened to the sunny day? The Weather Channel didn't mention any storms in the area.*

He looked around to see if he could paddle into a cove or someplace sheltered from the coming storm. No shelter in sight made him pull his life jacket even closer to his chest. *Thanks for the nag, Mom. I might need this today.*

A flash of light and a crack of thunder sent rain gushing down, and Charlie flinched. No way he was going to keep dry, even in his water-tight clothes. He reached under his seat and grabbed his sou'wester hat. Might keep his face dry and the water out of his eyes.

Maybe he should turn around and go back home? He looked back up the river towards his house. *Holy crap, how did the river get so high? I'll be lucky if the boat doesn't get swamped.* Judging from the wall of water behind him, he figured the storm must have started up near the river's piedmont origin.

To distract himself from his present danger, he thought of Katie. Charlie had finally gotten the courage to ask her to sit with him during lunch on Monday. And she'd said *yes!* Another reason to survive this storm.

A steady rhythm of paddling, first to the left and then to right, kept the kayak's nose sliding through the river. He was in control of the boat. It might feel kinda flimsy at the moment, but he knew it to be sturdy.

He shifted his weight backward from his hips to counter-act the flooding water raising the back of his kayak, trying to relax and go with the flow. Now he understood the full meaning of that phrase. The appearance of a church spire and the clock tower of New Bern's City Hall confirmed that he was close to the town. *Should be about a mile or so to the convergence of the Trent River.* Maybe that would slow the Neuse down. He sure hoped so. He didn't want to navigate under the Neuse River bridge at this speed. *Real easy to slam into a support pillar.*

As Charlie zipped under the railroad bridge that connected New Bern and Bridgeton, he saw the water cresting over the sea wall. There was definitely a chance of major flooding if the river didn't stop rising. His mind flashed a picture of the area after Hurricane Florence in 2018. *That couldn't happen again, could it?*

Emptying his mind of other things, Charlie looked toward the shore between Persimmon's Restaurant and the end of Pollock Street, hoping to steer there. But a microscopic turn to the right pushed the left side of his boat up. Like being on a rollercoaster going down a right-hand curve of its track. With his heart pounding in his chest, he figured he'd best press his left hip into the seat and turn the boat to the left. Remembering the sound of his dad's rumbling voice saying, "Good job, son, that did the trick," calmed Charlie down.

Seconds later movement from under the drawbridge to the right of Union Point Park caught his eye. There was a kayak heading into the Neuse from the Trent on a collision course. The paddler was looking away from him, unaware of the coming crash, he guessed. Charlie shouted, "Hey! Hey! Look out!"

She didn't turn her head, but the waves on the Neuse were lifting her prow as she tried to enter. The Trent's flow was much slower. The Neuse's current raised her kayak and slewed it sideways, tipping her into the water before it rolled keel up.

Charlie watched in horror as she disappeared beneath the surface. He paddled into the side of her capsized boat and grabbed a rope that bobbed to the surface at the bow. Figuring it to be the bow line, he held on tight, ignoring the searing pain as it ripped skin off his palm. *Knew I shoulda worn my gloves.* He reached his paddle over the keel of the boat and slowly pushed the two boats together in a parallel line.

He looked to the back, then to the sides, and finally to the fronts of both boats in hopes he'd see some sign of the girl. None! Not even a strand of her hair. Should he jump into the water? He shipped his paddle and reached for the buckle on his life vest but hesitated. *No sense both of us drowning.* The two boats slid through the water toward the Route 70 bridge. And as if the storm felt it had done enough damage, the wind eased up, and the sky lightened.

He looked over the side of the girl's kayak and thought he saw a hand reach out of the water. But before it could grab onto the keel, the water pushed it away.

He grabbed his paddle, and leaning over the upside-down boat as far as he dared, thrust it as straight down as far as possible. At first all he felt was the tug of the water. But then there was a sharp backward jerk. He stiffened his back muscles and yanked the paddle upward. First, he saw a hand. Then an arm and finally her head. He pulled the paddle toward himself, helping the gasping girl drape herself over the keel of her boat.

"Keep hold of my paddle until you catch your breath. I think we're heading to a small beach right by the bridge. I'll try to keep my body tilted that way."

The girl raised her head half an inch off the keel and nodded.

Charlie sucked in a surprised breath. *Is that Katie? Nah, she doesn't live down here.* But before he could say anything, the girl flopped her head back down, her breath still coming in gasps.

Charlie pushed his right knee against the side of his boat and twisted his torso to the right. He felt a slight shift in the kayaks' position. A few yards further on, he could feel a lessening of the current, and the small beach was closer.

The girl let go of the paddle and croaked out, "I'm fine. Start paddling."

Sounds like Katie. He pulled his paddle back and dipped it in the water on his left. Paddling forward from just the left side, he pushed the two boats to the little sandy beach.

The girl crawled onto the beach, stood, and tried to pull her kayak up, but a coughing fit doubled her over. She shivered in the stiff wind and slumped to the ground. Fortunately, the wind was pushing them closer to the sandy spit.

Seeing that her kayak is going to stay put, Charlie focused on getting them to the shore.

Charlie tested the water's depth with his paddle and realized it wasn't even knee-high for him. After beaching first his kayak and then hers, Charlie turned his attention to the girl huddled in a small bundle, her arms wrapped around her knees. *That is Katie.* He resisted enfolding her in his arms.

"Katie? Are you alright? What were you doing in the Trent River?"

She might have tried to smile, but coughed up more water instead. "I'm staying with Grandma Walker for a few days," she whispered.

Charlie sat beside her and touched her shoulder. "Can I put my arm around you? It might make you warm up faster."

She did smile this time as she nodded.

Charlie's body warmed up, too, as he put his arms around Katie. He rubbed his hands up and down her back and along her arms. "Does that help?

Katie nodded, and her shivering eased.

Charlie's first thought was about their lunch date on Monday, but knew it was not a priority right now.

"Will you be in school on Monday? Should I bring your schoolwork?"

Katie managed less of a croak. "A visiting nurse stays with Grandma until six, so I'll be in school."

Still not thinking that it was appropriate to say anything about sitting together at lunch, all Charlie could must was, "That's good."

Katie turned toward him and winked. "Besides, I don't want to miss our lunch date."

Charlie's heartbeat picked up; Katie had called it a date. "But how are you getting to school?"

Katie's smile took Charlie's breath away. "Oh, that's the surprise I was going to tell you about at lunch. I got my license two days ago, and Daddy bought me a car!"

"Wow, you are a lucky girl."

"It's called getting good grades, Charlie."

"Yeah, maybe I should try that, huh?"

Katie stroked his cheek and nodded.

"But it's so boring." He dug a toe into the sand. "I mean I get by just reading the book and listening to the teacher. But I've got better things to do than study for tests and things."

Katie frowned. "Not all of us are as smart as you."

Charlie wanted to hold her tighter. *Nah, that would freak her out. This girl stuff is hard.*

Katie rested her head on his shoulder.

I wonder if I should kiss her. He remembered the talk he'd had with his dad. "Take your time, son. Let her lead the way."

She moved even closer and kissed his cheek. "Thanks for saving me."

The kiss made his whole body jangle and a shiver run through him.

He turned to look at her. Maybe she wanted him to kiss her? He gently brushed his lips across hers.

She leaned into the kiss, increasing the contact between them.

That's a clear signal, right Dad? Charlie leaned toward her, not believing his luck.

A minute later, Katie inched back and smiled up at him. "That was awesome."

Charlie did manage a nod and squeaked out a "Yes."

Before he could pull her close again, another cough exploded out of her.

"Maybe we should get you back to your grandmother's. I'll call my mom to come get us."

"Yeah, but let me call my dad. He's office is just up the road and he's got a roof rack."

Charlie retrieved their waterproof bags from their kayaks' holds. "If your dad can't come, it won't take my mom long to come get us. She's working from home today." He sat beside Katie and pulled her close.

After Katie's dad said it would take him about ten minutes, Charlie said, "Well, while we're waiting tell me what your plans are after we graduate next year."

Katie smiled and sat up straighter. "I'm applying to UNC schools that have a graphic and fine arts degrees. Also, Elon University and Duke."

"I've seen some of your work at school and at Next Chapter Books & Arts." Charlie stroked Katie's arm and smiled. "You're good."

"Thanks. What do you want to do, Charlie? You're a good writer, and I love hearing you play the fiddle. Reminds me of Mark O'Connor."

"Wow, that's high praise!" Charlie pulled Katie close again and planted a sloppy kiss on her cheek.

She giggled but backed away. "We'd better get our kayaks up to the road." She brushed her lips across his cheek, heating up his blood again.

Katie started to pull her kayak up the hill, but slipped and sat down. "I guess I'm still worn out."

One after the other, Charlie pulled both kayaks to the road. Then he held out his hand and helped her up the hill. They huddled close until her dad pulled up.

When they were safely buckled into Mr. Walker's car, both in the back seat, Katie reached across the middle and grabbed Charlie's hand.

He smiled at her and said, "Thanks for picking us up, Mr. Kane."

"Thanks for saving Katie."

"It was just dumb luck." Safe and sound, Charlie chuckled. "But that was an awesome kayak ride!"

"Do you want to do that ever again?" asked Katie.

"Only the part where I rescued you." Charlie grinned from ear to ear.

Do Come In

The third issue came out in July of 2021 with theme of **Hospitality**. "Oh boy," thought I. "I've got just the story." My handsome devil and I love to give parties, and when we were much younger than we are now, we put on a Winter Holidays party. Since we have a lot of non-Christian friends, it seemed a bit rude to call our party a "Christmas" Party. So, we called it the "Winter Solstice" Party, instead.

Being the arrogant person that I am, I spent all of November cooking and freezing various recipes from my twenty-some cookbooks. Each year I chose a different cooking theme for the dishes, since I like to cook, or did back then. (I started cooking the family dinners in 1960 for my mother, my brother Bill, and his friend, who magically appeared just about dinner time most days.) I am now almost 82, and have gotten a bit lazy about cooking. And a few years back I got rid of all my cookbooks except my copy of *Fanny Farmers*, which my husband and I both use.

With the exception of my husband's crass partner, everybody came in his or her gussied up clothes and the women wore their best jewelry. This story is about the partner's, to me at least, very bad behavior. See what you think.

~

Jenna dabbed a smidge of cologne on her neck and wrists and, on the fourth try, latched the gold-chain bracelet with the jade stones on her wrist. She backed up to her husband, Daniel, for him to fasten the braided-gold necklace, dangling an oval-shaped emerald around her neck.

"Thanks for my birthday present, honey."

"You're welcome. Too bad we haven't been any place fancy enough for you to wear it before this." He squeezed her shoulder.

Jenna turned and smiled at him. "Our party isn't really that fancy, but I did want to show our friends what you'd given me." She slipped on her antique Lady's Rolex, his Christmas present from the year before. Glancing at the time, she gasped. "Dang, I'm running late."

Daniel frowned and checked his watch. "What's your hurry? We've got an hour before our guests are due to arrive."

She shook her head. "You forgot Katerina. She and Johnnie always come this early. Which means I have to be done, so I can entertain them."

"Why does she do that?"

"She thinks she's doing us a favor by coming early to help."

Daniel shrugged his shoulders. "Well, put her to work. I'll entertain Johnnie. He can help me set up the bar."

Jenna crinkled the side of her mouth. "I was raised to be in hostess mode when the guests start to arrive. I can't ask her to help. My mother's voice always says for me to stop working and just be the best hostess." She opened their bedroom door, smoothing her pale-green blouse and slim black slacks. "But this time I'm ready for her. She can help put things out."

Just as she shut the bedroom door, the doorbell rang, and their Llewellyn Setter, Ashley, announced their guests' arrival. Jenna stopped at the bottom of the stairs and pasted a smile on her face. *I love giving this party, and Katerina does mean well.*

She opened the door and grinned. "Oh my, Katerina, don't you look lovely."

Katerina blushed and twirled to show how the clear-glass beads dotting the turquoise dress twinkled in the overhead light. "This is the fanciest party we go to all year," she said as her eyes sparkled with joy.

Jenna bowed her head at the compliment. She hugged Johnnie and lightly kissed his cheek. "I can always rely on you making sure we're ready before hand." She shut the door behind them just as Daniel came down the stairs.

"Hey, Johnnie. You're just in time to help me set up the bar." He turned to Katerina and kissed her cheek. "Hello to you. Jenna beat you to the punch. I don't think there's much for you to help with." He winked at his wife. "But maybe she'll find something."

"I really do mean to help," Katerina said.

Jenna nodded. "I know you do, dear, but I was always told to be ready in plenty of time. You can help me put the rest of the food in the oven to heat up. In about thirty minutes, we'll start putting out the cheeses and veggies and the shrimp." She smiled at her friends.

"What's the food theme this year?" Katerina asked. "I love seeing what you've planned each time."

"I decided on dumplings from around the world. At least two thirds of my cookbooks have recipes for them. I've got Asian pot stickers, Hispanic empanadas, and Slavic perogies, to name a few." She turned toward the kitchen. "I love trying out the various styles."

The friends worked together setting out the treats in the places Ashley couldn't reach. "We'll wait until other people have arrived before I put out stuff where he can get at it."

"Are you putting the food for the Kosher Keepers in the family room as usual?" Katerina asked, as she watched Jenna take out the challah for the Kosher Corner.

Jenna stood for a second, but then said, "You know what? I think I'll set up the Corner in the living room this year, just to get people mingling more."

"Good idea. What can I do now?" asked Katerina.

Jenna took a quart of whipping cream out of the refrigerator. "Please whip the cream for the other cakes. But when you've finished just leave the beater and bowl standing. Daniel will need it for the eggnog."

Daniel and Charlie came into the kitchen just as their wives had finished heating up the last dishes. "Is it okay for me to put the finishing touches on the eggnog now?" Daniel raised his eyebrows at Jenna.

She waved her hand toward the counter where the beater was sitting, still dripping bits of whipped cream into the now-empty bowl. "All yours, your whipping cream is in the fridge."

She nodded at Katerina. "I think it's time for us to have our sampling of the dishes now. The rest of the guests will be here in about ten minutes or so." She handed her friend a paper plate. "I gotta have my share of the shrimp before Helena gets here for her yearly non-Kosher indulgence."

The friends had finished their sampling of the goodies, when the doorbell rang. "Well, with your generous help, m'dear," Jenna said, patting her friend's shoulder, "We're ready to party."

Katerina smiled. "Glad to help. But let's party!"

"The work did go faster," Jenna said, giving her friend a hug.

The guests came in a steady stream with ladies dressed in pretty cocktail outfits and the men with slacks and dress shirts. Some of them just came on in without knocking or ringing the doorbell. Jenna would get a tap on the shoulder and turn to greet friends.

When Ari and Ruth arrived, Jenna grabbed them by the hands. "Good to see you. The challah turned out especially well this year, but please do wander around to meet other of our guests. And I found a Jewish dumpling recipe that's a bit more flavorful than the usual matzo balls. I'll see you at 'Kosher Corner.'"

About forty minutes into the party, the doorbell rang. Daniel looked at Jenna and raised his eyebrows. "Who's missing?"

Jenna shrugged her shoulders, "Might be Beatrice and Jacob. They're frequently late. Jacob does love to make a grand entrance." She headed to the front door with a welcome smile pasted on her face. *Don't let Jacob get to you this time*, she thought. But when she opened the door, her mouth dropped in surprise. Or was it horror? Or rage? Jacob was wearing a railroad engineer's uniform, complete with the accompanying the tall, crowned and visored striped hat. Beatrice was dressed in a lovely rose-colored dress and nice jewelry. *How she puts up with him, I don't know*, Jenna thought.

Daniel had come up behind her and gently moved her aside. "Honey, I think you left something simmering on the stove."

Jenna nodded, smiled at their guests, and said, "That's a beautiful dress, Beatrice. I'll chat with you later, but I'd better rescue the dumpling sauce."

Thankful for her husband's tact in keeping her from whacking Jacob upside the head for his thoughtlessness, she headed up to her bedroom, muttering to herself. "Calm down, calm down. He's a guest in our house, so if he wants to be his boorish self, it's his right."

Minutes later she was relaxed enough to hurry to the kitchen. "Of course, respecting our efforts would never cross his mind," she muttered. She turned off the stove, poured the sauce into a waiting container, and waited until her pasted-on smile became a real one.

As she headed back to the dumplings with the sauce, Jenna noticed that Helena had moved on from her stand by the shrimp. "Happy?" Jenna asked.

Helena laughed. "Oh yeah. I even left some for others."

"I think God will allow you this one indulgence, don't you?" Jenna moved on to see what dishes needed replenishing and whether all the food was at the right temperature, replacing used up Sterno containers and chatting with her guests.

About three hours into the party, she and Daniel met up in the kitchen. "We're running out of main dishes," she said. "Could you start the coffee and tea, while I put out the desserts?" She left her husband in the kitchen setting up the hot-drinks area as she took her *pièce de résistance*, a bûche de Noël, out of the refrigerator. It was one of her favorite recipes from her ancient copy of Julia Child's *French Chef* cookbook. She loved the way the special meringue/chocolate-buttercream icing spread in waves over a simple orange jelly-roll cake making it really look like a yule log. She looked at the crowded dessert-filled table and decided to put the cake elsewhere.

Katerina was sitting on the family-room sofa chatting with Jacob, who hadn't even taken his engineer's hat off. She was sure there were enough people around that Ashley, who had a taste for people food, wouldn't be able to eat it.

"Oh goodie," said Katerina, "I was wondering if I'd be quick enough this year to get a piece."

"Please don't let the dog near it." Jenna put the dessert plates next to the cake and cut the first slice. "Enjoy."

She'd almost completed another circle amongst her friends when she noticed her dog with what looked like a mushroom sticking out of his mouth, proudly walk into the living room. "Ashley, give me that, you bad dog." She looked closer and realized it was one of the meringue mushrooms from Yule Log. She rushed back into the family room just in time to see Jacob, almost breathless with laughter, watch as Katerina served the last piece of cake to another guest. She had tears rolling down her cheeks she was laughing so hard.

"What's so funny?" Jenna always loved a good joke.

Katerina stifled her giggles, and her eyes took on a wary look. "Nothing. Just a joke."

Jacob continued to guffaw, but pulled himself together enough to say, "Well, Ashley licked the cake from one end to the other before anyone could have a piece."

Jenna's mouth flew open, and her face slowly turned bright pink. "Why didn't you stop him?"

"Why?" Jacob sputtered out between laughs.

"Oh, it's alright, honey. We just called people over to eat the cake before the dog did," Katerina said.

Mouth open in shock, Jenna snatched up the plate and marched into the kitchen without a word. *How could Katerina do that? Jacob I can understand, jerk that he is, but Katerina? She knows how hard I work on this party.*

She figured her best bet was to avoid both of them for the rest of the party. She didn't know if she could be the good hostess otherwise.

The party finally ended about the time Jenna felt she couldn't stand on her cramping feet another minute. She was proud of herself for having avoided Jacob for the rest of the evening. But she'd had to paste on a smile when Katerina came and apologized. "Jacob can be a bad influence."

The next morning, just as Jenna was wiping the counters down again, Ruth called to express her thanks for another nice party. She said how much she appreciated Jenna's always putting the Kosher Corner in the same place so the food was always acceptable for Ruth to eat. "I don't know what I'd do if you ever moved the corner."

Oops, thought Jenna, but she didn't say anything. "I'm always happy to see you. Oh, I didn't get a chance to ask how you're enjoying being a rabbi."

"Thanks for asking. I enjoy it immensely, but it is hard work."

"I bet, but as long as it's fulfilling, go for it."

Just as Jenna hung up, Daniel came in from walking Ashley. "Ruth called to thank us for the party," Jenna shook her head and smiled before saying, "turns out she didn't realize that I'd put her Corner in the living room. But I figure what she doesn't know won't hurt her, and I don't think God will strike her dead for eating forbidden food." But she wondered if Ruth had thought it strange that there was no challah there.

"God's a bit more forgiving of our mistakes than we are. Oh, and speaking of mistakes, we should be a bit more careful about what we allow Ashley to eat during our parties. His gut is messed up today."

"Definitely the last time I put desserts on the coffee tables," Jenna said, stifling the urge to call both Jacob and Katerina up and yell at them about what they'd done last night.

Her husband hugged her before settling in for a long kiss. When he pulled away, he said, "Thank you for throwing such a good party, Babe."

"It's your doing as much as mine, honey," she answered.

"Well, you do all the work."

Jenna stroked his hand, "But you're the one who makes everyone feel at home."

"We make a good team," Daniel said and kissed her cheek. "Speaking of that, I saw you looked like you were going to kill Jacob whenever you got close to him. And you didn't look to happy with Katerina. What was that all about?"

Jenna told her husband what had happened. "That's probably why Ashley is feeling sick today. Chocolate is poisonous to dogs."

"Boor that he is, I will miss him as a work partner." Charlie said. "The good news is Jacob's leaving the firm and moving to Charlottesville at the end of this year,"

"Works for me." Jenna smiled at her husband and sat down with her cup of tea. Even with the "Ashley and the cake" incident, she chalked the party up as another success.

Rosie the Riveter

If I remember correctly, **History** was the theme of edition #4, and I was hoping to extend my publishing feat to four issues of the magazine.

My mother had a hard-but-rewarding adult life. This story is about her time as a "Rosie the Riveter" model during WWII. (If you don't know who the "Rosies" were, do check them out at https://guides.loc.gov › rosie-the-riveter. Now, obviously I can't know how Mother felt about her life, but she did always show us a happy side.

WWII was tough for us, for our country, and for the world in general, but perhaps we suffered more than most. I was born on May 29th, 1941, the night before my father, Captain Thompson Brooke Maury III, was due to go to the Philippines where he was stationed on Bataan. My maternal grandfather, Colonel Paul Delmont Bunker, was already there as second-in-command of Corregidor. Both of them died as prisoners of war.

This story tells a bit about Mother's life during and after the war. The story also appears, in part, as a chapter in my third novel, *Earthquakes,* published in 2020.

~

Priscilla wiped her eyes one last time. "Stop feeling sorry for yourself," she said and gave herself a stern look in the mirror. "You can't let your children see you mourn." She brushed her platinum-blond hair and put on her make up—gray pencil along her eyebrows and gray mascara on her lashes, plus a hint of light pink rouge on her cheeks to brighten her face. "There, now people can see me, and I'm ready to tackle my new job as Lockheed's first female Tool & Die designer. Not exactly chemistry, but getting there."

"Wish you were alive to brag about your wife, my darling Brooke." A smile brightened her face as she conjured up the image of her husband, her brother Paul, and her father standing side by side on a cloud beaming and pointing her out to all the other angels who happened by. In her mind war was an evil thing. She'd lost Paul in 1935, not because of war exactly, but still he was flying a plane carrying a bomb.

In December 1943, her father died of malnutrition in a Japanese POW camp in the Philippines. Brooke had survived the Bataan Death March, but not the Japanese going against the Geneva Convention. They crowded her husband and other POWs onto unmarked ships heading to Japan. Unsuspecting Allied Forces sank all four of the ships. Brooke, champion swimmer though he was, drowned while he tried to save another man. His body would forever rest at the bottom of Subic Bay.

She shook her head to clear the glum thoughts and slipped into Sally's room, where her youngest child was having her morning nap. She brushed her lips along her daughter's shiny red hair, hoping the three-year-old wouldn't awaken. The thought that Sally would never know her father made Priscilla tear up again. Never would any of them see darling Brooke until they met in Heaven. Priscilla forced a smile; at least they'd had six years together.

She passed through the kitchen to see if the maid had all she needed to do her job and left through the side door to get to her car, a present from her remaining sibling, Bill.

When she got to work, the manager called her into his office. "Priscilla, how's your new job working out? Do you have any questions about the work? Do you need any help?"

"Thanks, Mr. Donohue, but I think I've got it all figured out. I'm really enjoying the work."

"You're quite smart for a woman," he said. "Guess you'd have to be to attend MIT."

Priscilla smiled and thought about what not to say. She wouldn't ask him why he thought women were not as smart as men. Or how women could not only do all the domestic work and also be chemists or engineers or doctors. "Thank you, sir. Well, I'd best get started."

"Wait, there is one other thing."

"Yes?" she said, turning from the door.

Mr. Donohue came from behind his desk to stand close to her. "Remember when the press came and took your picture? And wrote a story about you're being selected to represent our company as a Rosie the Riveter. It's quite an honor."

"I do, sir. And I am proud to represent our company and our country, but you still haven't told me what I'm supposed to do." She smiled at her boss, not wishing to offend him. "I spend enough time away from my children as it is."

She thought about the trouble her oldest child, Richard, had gotten into just recently. If she'd been at home she would have at least known where he was going. Now he was having to work for the neighborhood gardener to pay some for the damage he and his friends had done jumping through walls and floors in an under-construction office building. Plus, he'd might have a police record. Priscilla still pictured the builder coming to her in tears. He'd lost his life savings since the country was just emerging from the Great Depression.

And Anne, her next oldest, ended up breaking her arm falling out of a tree a year before that. Plus, Bill, at five, had fallen into the incinerator pit in the back yard. Fortunately, there had been no fire going. Just this past week the doctor finally pronounced Sally over German measles complications with pneumonia. Sometimes Priscilla wondered if she was a bad mother.

"Priscilla? Are you still with me?" Mr. Donohue encircled her arm with his hand.

"Oh, sorry sir, I was thinking about my children."

"To answer your question, you'll have to do some work promoting the war effort. Collecting used rubber and broken metal things, but you may take your children along. And, of course, a photographer will accompany you."

"I suppose we can make it an adventure."

"That's the spirit. I knew you'd be a 'go-to' girl." Mr. Donohue smiled and squeezed her shoulders. "Your first assignment is this Saturday at the Navy Yard. You'll be christening and launching one of the first-ever modern aircraft carriers. It's going to carry some of our planes. Wear your prettiest dress, something to highlight your nice figure and pretty face. Too bad the photo won't be in color to show your pretty blue eyes."

Priscilla stepped to the side to get out of her boss's embrace as she said, "And especially my children's red hair. What time do we have to be there, sir?"

"Five o'clock in the afternoon. We'll send a car to pick you up."

"Thank you, Mr. Donohue. I hope there will be enough room for my mother, since she'll want to come if she's not doing something for the Red Cross." Priscilla left her boss's office before he could grab her again.

Saturday came and the family, all dressed in their Sunday finest, piled into the car. The boys wore their best suits; Priscilla noting she'd have to buy Richard a new one soon. She had splurged on a new hat for herself.

At the Navy Yard, an admiral addressed the crowd, droning on about how exciting it was to launch a new ship and what an honor it was to have a Rosie the Riveter there to christen it.

"Why couldn't he just hand the bottle of champagne to Mom so she can smash it?" muttered Richard.

Finally, the admiral gave the bottle to Priscilla, stretching taut the long, shiny blue ribbon fastened to the bow of the ship. She reached her arm back and hurled the champagne forward. "Clunk," went the bottle when it hit the hull and bounced backward undamaged.

Priscilla grabbed it again and hurled the bottle forward even harder. Another clunk, another failed attempt. People in the audience chuckled, which made her neck and face turn red. She felt as if her scalp had turned red as well. Again, Priscilla grabbed the bottle and pulled it back, but this time she backed up three steps, frowning in concentration. She twisted her torso away from the ship and then stepped forward as if pitching a strike at a batter, letting her back leg step forward and right arm release toward the bow.

KAPOW! Champagne flew everywhere, as did tiny shards of glass. The crowd roared out a cheer, and everyone on the stage quickly backed up trying to dodge the mess. After being presented with a bouquet of flowers that almost covered her torso. Priscilla grinned from ear-to-ear and posed for her picture. She beckoned for her children and mother to join her and introduced them to the admiral.

A photographer approached the group and said, "Excuse me, could I have you all stand by the carrier so I can take your picture?" He had Priscilla stand directly under the bow of the ship with her family clustered around her. She felt like she was a miniature of herself, the ship was so big.

When the ceremony and picture taking were done, they had dinner at the famous Brown Derby, which, as usual, was filled with actors and actresses, plus as many gawkers as had been able to get reservations. The food was good, as was the service, and it was fun to check out the celebrities. They even saw Montgomery Cliff off by himself in a dark corner.

The following Monday, as Priscilla walked Bill to school, he pointed at a new billboard. "Look Mommy, there we are at the launching."

When she read the ad copy under their photo saying she gave her children a particular type of cereal she'd never even heard of, Priscilla gasped. "How dare they use us like that!" She wrote down the information so she could contact the company, and when she got to work, she went straight to Mr. Donohue's office to complain.

His secretary said, "That's awful. I'll tell him when he gets back from his meeting."

The next evening her boss greeted her when she got to work, "Oh, Priscilla," he said, "I didn't think you'd mind. Our company gets publicity from this and a little money."

"What about me? Do I get any money? And I don't want my children's picture up there for the world to see. Please take it down." She frowned and shook her head. "I haven't even heard of the cereal, let alone tasted it."

"Well, it's just one advertisement, my dear."

"Take it down as soon as possible. It's wrong."

The next week, Bill pointed out that the billboard was changed. "Good," said Priscilla. "I wasn't sure if Mr. Donohue would listen to me." Priscilla smiled and stroked Bill's head. She didn't say how glad she was that her boss hadn't fired her for insubordination or something.

Priscilla's job at Lockheed and her Rosie the Riveter duties ended when the war did. Returning soldiers and sailors would need their jobs back to support their families. Nobody seemed to notice that she had to support her family, too.

She wrote to her long-time friend, Margaret Kelly, in 1947 as a continuance of their long-standing correspondence.

> *Dear Margaret,*
>
> *Congratulations on being awarded your PhD in biochemistry. I always enjoyed studying at George Washington University with you and your sister Mary, but am also glad to have studied at MIT when Daddy was transferred to a nearby army base. As I've mentioned before, I loved being in Boston and going to free dress rehearsals for the Boston Symphony.*
>
> *I am hoping you can help me find a job in the District of Columbia or Maryland or Virginia, where I can work as a chemist and get the children out of what I consider a bad place to raise them.*

Margaret wrote back urging her to come to Maryland and take a job at the newly started Cancer-Chemotherapy Research Center for the National Institutes of Health. Priscilla jumped at the chance, happy to get away from the glitz of Los Angeles. She retired from NIH thirty years later.

"Time for me to focus on my painting and sculpting," she said. She was actually quite good at that.

Georgie Counts Her Blessings

The fifth theme was **Blessings**, which fit quite well for my view of the world. All of us have heartbreak of some sort or other along our time from birth to death and we must find our own ways of coping with the sadness. My husband and I lost our oldest child in an accident, a sorrow we will carry always. But we do find ways of coping and finding joy even as we muddle along with our lives. One of our ways of coping is to remember the joy and "blessings" we found riding the horses our daughter left us with. Riding a horse is indeed good for one's soul anyway.

~

Georgie slipped the bit out of Rippy's mouth, glad she'd used the special bridle/halter equipment on this trail ride. From the start, her plan was to stop by her favorite stream just to hear the water washing all her fears and sadness downstream.

Rippy lowered his silky black muzzle to munch on the succulent, pale-green grass growing at the stream's edge amongst the watercress and moss. A simple blessing for him, Georgie felt. Confident he wouldn't wander far with so much to eat, she dropped one rein, wrapped the other around the saddle horn, and loosened his girth a notch.

After a final pat on Rippy's black rump, Georgie settled herself on a bed of leaves and leaned back against a fallen tree trunk, feeling the smooth Sycamore bark gently scratch an itch on her back. She closed her eyes and listened to the stream trickle over moss-covered rocks. It bubbled from one slight drop in elevation to the next on its way to the river a half-mile away.

Sunlight warmed her shoulders as it filtered through breaks in the oak and sycamore trees, and she breathed a contented sigh as peace seeped into her soul. She could feel the burden of life's latest disappointments lifting. After all, she wasn't the only author whose work had been rejected. She chuckled as all the famous authors who had survived countless rejections came to mind. And Georgie's latest rejections hadn't even been because of the editors. Instead, it was the marketers—the money men—who had rejected the stories because they already had similar ones in the works.

"Yeah, Rippy," she explained to her horse, "At least the editors liked my writing. They both asked for more stories from me."

Rippy just continued his grazing, but he did cock an ear backward to listen to her.

Now, there was a blessing Georgie could count on every day. The joy she felt when she was working with their horses. And the connection she felt to the daughter she and her husband had lost years earlier.

The memory of how happy their daughter Susanne had always been working with her horses made Georgie smile. She remembered Susanne's phone call. "Hey, Georgie and Dad, come see my wedding gift from Gary. He's all black, except for a star on his forehead and white socks above his hooves." And how gently she'd gotten shy Rippy to accept her and then to allow people to ride him. Susanne always said she was blessed to have a good husband and her horse.

Georgie thought back on the past forty years, remembering that the many good times outnumbered all the bad ones. She smiled at the memory of her first meeting with her husband. When he'd announced that he had four children to raise, she'd laughed and said, "Oh, an instant family!" She was sure she'd be up to the task. She felt blessed when they'd learned to love each other.

Now, the ever-deepening love she had for her husband and he for her brought such joy. With each passing year she'd felt a stronger bond with him. The biggest blessing of all.

Georgie's body relaxed another group of muscles with each remembrance. Blessed peace spread through her soul.

The sun peeked through openings in the canopy above her, warming her face and glistening off Rippy's blue-black coat. Soon they'd have to head back home to the other duties of the day. But now that she was ready, newly energized and at peace with herself along with the world, she looked forward to her day.

Fairy Toothbrushes

Illustration by Brooklynn Moore

The theme for the issue was **Gifts**. And did I have the story for it! Last year I had to have another root canal, not a whole lot of fun, as you can imagine, but the dentist who did the surgery is a delightful fellow, an avid reader, and a writer. He was very descriptive about what he was doing in my mouth, which I found to be comforting.

But when he said, "Now I'm taking a tiny toothbrush to clean out the inside of your tooth," I started mentally plotting a story about a fairy with a very small toothbrush. Of course, I couldn't say anything right then since he had all kinds of things in my mouth.

When he finally gave me a chance to speak, I said, "Thanks Doctor, I'm imagining a fairy-sized toothbrush. So, allow me to introduce Bernadetta Stuart, DDS.

~

Bernadetta Stuart folded her tiny wings and watched from the grass as various shoes walked by her. She shook her head at the shiny brown shoes with no laces that thumped like a herd of elephants. *Boring.* After all, Fairies do like glamor.

She shook her head at the bare-arched sandals that slip-slopped along with only a strap between toes to hold them on. The wearer might feel even something as small as a fairy hitching a ride up the stairs.

Feet after feet marched past, but then came a person wearing dark-blue trainers with turquoise laces. *Perfect.* The laces matched Bernadetta's eyes. As a disguise, she grabbed a small bit of dandelion fluff and hopped on for a ride into the dentist's office. Up the front steps to porch and then through the front door.

She could have flown up the stairs, but maybe someone would see her and shriek about a bug flying into the building. After all, most people didn't see or even believe in Fairies.

But this dentist was a very a special person. He not only believed in fairies; he saved a special gift for her every week.

She rode the shoe into the room where Dr. Williams's waited for his patient, and as the woman settled herself in the dentist's chair, the doctor's assistant leaned down to move the fluff carrying Bernadetta from the patient's shoe.

"Oh dear," said the assistant, "let me clean up your shoe." With light fingers, she also dropped about a foot of dental floss into the fairy's hand.

Bernadetta smiled at the young woman and looped the floss around the drawer pull of the lowest drawer. To keep the patient from seeing her, the fairy decided it would be better to climb the cabinet drawers until she reached the top of the doctor's work bench. The tiniest drop of honey sat in a small water cup for Bernadetta to snack on until her friends were done with the patient.

"We'll see you in six weeks, Ms. Walker. And we'll finish up with a temporary crown," the doctor said, as he helped his patient out of the dentist chair. "Remember not to eat anything hot for the next two hours."

"Thank you, Doctor Williams, but before I go, may I know the name of the fairy who hitched a ride on my shoe? And also why she came here in the first place?"

"Ah, and here we thought we were being so sneaky." He held out his left pinky finger to his tiny visitor. Bernadetta hopped onto it. After holding his finger out to Ms. Walker, he said, "Ms. Walker, allow me to introduce you to Dr. Bernadetta Stuart."

"Doctor Bernadetta? Why Doctor Williams, she's just a fairy."

The fairy stamped her foot and scowled at the woman. "Just a fairy! Just a fairy, you say."

"Ooops," said the patient. "I didn't know Fairies did anything but make magic and dance around toadstools in the full moon."

"Well, somebody needs to take care of our teeth, wouldn't you think?"

"I'm so sorry. They don't teach things like that in fairytales."

"Hmmph," snorted Bernadetta, "A lot you know."

"You're right about that, Doctor. I find I know less and less the older I get. Anyway, I do hope you'll forgive me."

Bernadetta's frown disappeared and instead her lips curled up as if she might smile.

Ms. Walker went to pay her bill, hoping she'd see Bernadetta again. She was almost out the front door when an idea came to her. She said to the check-out fellow, "I'm sorry, Henry, I had one more thing I wanted to ask Dr. Williams. Is that alright?"

Henry nodded. "You're his last patient of the day, so help yourself."

When she got back to the patient room, the good dentist was standing by his storage chest talking to Bernadetta, who was describing a procedure she had done on one of her patients. "Your toothbrushes that you use inside the tooth are perfect for getting in between the teeth. How can I pay you back?"

"No need. Those are my gift to you."

Ms. Walker tapped lightly on the door. "Excuse me for intruding, but I would like to do a favor for Doctor Bernadetta to make up for being so rude."

"Thank you, kind madam, but that's not necessary," said the fairy.

"I'm here to offer you a ride down the stairs on my shoe, if you'd like."

Bernadetta smiled and shook Doctor Williams' little finger. "I am ready to go, so I will take you up on your kind offer, Ms. Walker. Perhaps I can do a favor for you someday."

"Just knowing a fairy is favor enough for me." The kind woman held out her right pinkie to the fairy and lowered her to the glorious blue trainer with the turquoise shoelace.

The gift of a new friendship was lovely.

Afterword

The next theme is Food! So, my brain is happily churning with ideas to write about food. And I hope to extend my short-story publishing streak to the seventh issue of Next Chapter Literary Magazine. You can find copies of the magazine for sale at Next Chapter Books and Art, 320 S. Front Street, New Bern, NC 28560; or https://thenextchapternc.com.

They are also available through Amazon.

Acknowledgements

Writing in some ways is a solitary pursuit, since authors do have to isolate themselves to concentrate on telling the story in written words.

I have many people critique my work to tell me where I've missed mistakes. This particular set of stories is the product of Michelle Garren Flye's prompts for stories to publish in her *Next Chapter Literary Magazine*. So, thanks for being my publisher and my friend.

Thanks also to my ever-supportive but honest husband followed by my encouraging family and friends.

And then we come to the members of my three critique groups. All intriguing writers themselves. Linda Burke, Ed Hall, Veronica Krug, Ann LePere, Carol Lunney-Hampson, Barbara McCreary, Jill Olson, Anechy Padron, Mila Pompadour, Loretta Potts, and Stanley Trice. Thanks to all you clever and supportive people.

The illustrator whose pencil drawings illustrate the first and last stories, is eleven-year-old Brooklynn Moore. Be sure to look for her as she progresses in her journey as an artist.

And, finally, to our young cat, Pandie, who reminds me that feeding her should always take precedent over writing stories.

About the Author

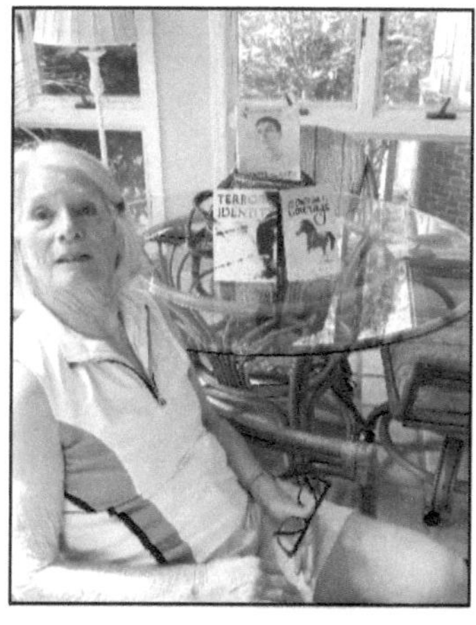

Generally, Sarah Maury Swan writes novels for children between the ages of 8 and 18, though many a "grown up" has enjoyed reading them. This is her first collection of short stories, but not her last. She's already planning her second collection.

When people ask her where she's from, her answer usually is a horse farm in Maryland. Still, that's not the whole answer. She was born at Ft. Lewis, Washington, but left there with her mother and three siblings when she was ten days old. After six years in Los Angeles, CA, where her mother worked at Lockheed, the family moved to Garrett Park, MD, her home until she married her husband. She, her husband, and his four children moved to Jacksonville, AL, where they worked at becoming a family. Two years later they moved back to Maryland and lived in Bethesda, Columbia, and finally Granite, MD.

She and her handsome devil now live outside the delightful town of New Bern, NC. All the moving has added reality to her stories.

Her books are available at the Next Chapter Books & Art store at 320 S. Front Street, New Bern, NC, but also through her website, https://sarahmauryswanlovesbooks.com and at https://www.amazon.com/s?k=sarah+maury+swan. Her third novel, *Earthquakes*, is available through https://IngramSpark.com.

www.ingramcontent.com/pod-product-compliance
Lightning Source LLC
Chambersburg PA
CBHW021751190726
48290CB00008B/2568